NIFFTY

TO THE SEA

Written by
Randy Lee

Illustrated by
Josh Ebert

This book belongs to

_____

Published by Orange Hat Publishing 2020
ISBN 978-1-64538-173-0

For information, please contact:

Orange Hat Publishing
www.orangehatpublishing.com
Waukesha, WI

To my son, Cruz, who changed my life and made me become a man. This book is an example of how you can truly do anything you put your mind to and work for. "I can't" doesn't exist. Dreams can become reality.

To my daughter, Cecilia, who came after. I love you so much, and I know you will reach the stars.

To their mother, Irma, who is responsible for the two greatest gifts of all. Thank you for all your support.

My name is

NIFFTY

and I belong to

THE SEA.

Did you know it was made
for you and for me?

I'm leaving today,
as soon as I

CAN!

I can travel by air
or travel by

LAND.

I have to admit,
I'm a little

AFRAID.

It's too far to walk

in the shoes that I

MADE.

I thought I could travel
on the back of a

DOG.

But when I jumped on,
he leapt at a

FROG!

I'll try a train next;
I think that'd be

SMART.

But the train hit a bump
and the carts split

APART!

I'm bouncing in the palm
of a big brown

BEAR.

Oh great, he just stopped
to comb his

HAIR!

It's much harder
than I thought
to get to the

SEA.

But my name is Niffty
and it belongs to

ME!

I almost forgot something
I wanted to try,
So I grabbed my kite
and started to fly!
Flying on my kite had been
working out well
Until it got caught on a truck
delivering mail.
"I know I can get there,"
I thought.

"JUST TRY!"

And then I noticed
something up in the sky.
Soaring through the clouds,
it was amazing to see
My favorite superhero
flying down to help me!
He put me on his back,
and I said, "Off to the sea!
I'm Niffty, and
it's waiting for

ME!"

Soon we were soaring over
a great stretch of water,
And he put me down gently
on a duck made of rubber.
"I made it!" I thought
as the duck bobbed and swayed,
And we laughed and splashed
all day as we

PLAYED.

Suddenly a voice yelled
out loud and clear,

"BATH TIME
IS OVER,
TIME TO
DRY OFF,
DEAR."

My name is Niffty
and I belong to the sea.
I am a bath toy,
and that's my best friend Cruzie!
We love bath time and make-believe,
so we imagine the tub is

A SEA JUST FOR ME.

Bath time has been fun,
but it's time for

BED.

Turn the page
to find the toys
from the story

YOU JUST
READ!

colorme!